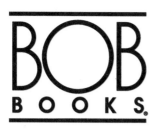

The New Puppy

by LYNN MASLEN KERTELL
illustrated by SUE HENDRA

SCHOLASTIC INC.

New York   Toronto   London   Auckland

Sydney   Mexico City   New Delhi   Hong Kong

ISBN 978-0-545-38268-7

12 11 10 9 8 7 6 5 4 3 2 1   12 13 14 15 16/0

Printed in the U.S.A.
First printing, January 2012   40

Jack and Anna want a puppy.

A puppy is a friend.

A puppy likes to play.

"A puppy is a lot of work,"
say Mom and Dad.

"Puppies need to be fed," says Dad.

"Puppies need to go out," says Mom.

"We will take care of it,"
the kids say.

Jack and Anna can do a
good job.

There are many dogs at the pet shelter.

Big dogs, small dogs,
fluffy dogs, shaggy dogs.

Jack and Anna like
the brown puppy.

The puppy gives Anna a kiss.

"What will you name your pet?"
asks Mom.

"We can call him Buddy!"
says Jack.

Buddy loves to chase a ball.

He loves to tug a rope.

Jack and Anna want to draw.

Buddy wants to help.

Jack and Anna make a fort.

Buddy jumps in.

"Time to go out," says Mom.

Buddy runs and runs.

Anna gives Buddy his dinner.

Jack gives him water.

Buddy is tired.

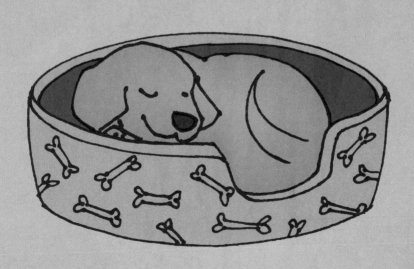

Buddy falls fast asleep.

Tomorrow, Buddy will be ready
to play again.

again	asleep
care	chase
dinner	friend

Buddy falls fast **asleep**.

Buddy will play **again**.

Buddy loves to **chase** a ball.

We will take **care** of a dog.

A puppy is a **friend**.

Anna gives Buddy his **dinner**

help	kiss
loves	out
puppy	want

The puppy gives Anna a **kiss**.

Buddy wants to **help**.

Time to go **out**.

He **loves** to tug a rope.

Jack and Anna **want** a puppy.

Jack and Anna like the brown **puppy**.